Vale
Thomas

Out of the Shadows

A Novelette by   John S Peters

This Book is dedicated to my loving wife and constant companion.

Table of contents

Chapter 1

The days were getting longer and winter's icy grip on the prairies was broken at the last. The snow was melting fast and the purple crocuses and bluebells were a welcome sight. I could hear the ebb and flow of the traffic below the window of my second floor apartment.

I guess I must've stared at the ceiling for another five minutes trying to decide whether I should get up and face the day, or if I should close my eyes and sleep for another hour. When I opened my eyes again I knew by the clock on the wall that another two hours had gone by. I was never sure why I liked this clock.

Maybe it was because of the songbirds which were pictured on the face, and may be it was because the clock actually worked and played a different bird song on every hour.

I had found it at a garage sale the summer before, and after cleaning it properly I found that it actually worked as it was meant to. I don't know about you, but for me there is something to be said about waking up to the singing of birds.

Rolling out of bed was easy. I had been in a hurry when I moved into this apartment, and decided to dispense with the bed frame.

I found it to be cumbersome and annoying. A large square of carpeting on the floor to protect the hardwood, the queen-size box spring on top of that, followed by the mattress. Which meant of course, that falling out of bed didn't hurt quite so much.

Finding this apartment had been a real godsend. Eight hundred square feet, all hardwood flooring, two large bedrooms, a decent kitchen, and a good-sized bathroom with an old cast-iron tub.

It was all a young man like myself could ask for, at $500 monthly. The old style boiler in the basement of the building kept all 20 suites toasty warm on the coldest days.

The walls were lathe and plaster, which meant that I did not hear the neighbors as much as I would have somewhere else. The walls had been painted a greenish blue color which was not too hard on the eyes, and so I did not bother to paint it over when I moved in.

Somebody had blessed me with a beautiful mahogany colored stereo console, with a color TV screen which was either 32 inches or 36.

I really can't remember and I don't care really, it was big enough. I had a beautiful futon bed which doubled as a couch, and two reddish brown leather La-Z-Boy recliner's which I had also found while I was bargain-hunting at the local garage sales. They had been asking for $100 for the pair or $75 each, but I got the pair for $80. Cable TV was included in the rent as was the water. That left only power to pay for, which was not too hard to take.

Making my way to the kitchen I checked to see if there was water in my stovetop kettle, and then turned the electric burner on high. While I was waiting for her to boil I took care of the bathroom necessities according to the order of priorities. After shaving and drying my face with the hand towel designated for that purpose, I heard the kettle begin to sing, and took care of the next priority which was coffee!

For me instant coffee was all the same. Whether Folgers, Maxwell House, or Nabob, it all depended on convenience, availability, and most importantly cash money. This had been a good month and so today it was Folger's coffee. After adding cream and sugar to taste, I glanced toward the doorway were several envelopes had been pushed under, and I took a moment to collect them and return to the table.

One was from the church, the other five were from people who had been at the service of the previous night at the Healing Centre Church. Toward the end of the service Pastor Marshall had made an announcement that God had open some doors for me in the States, and that anyone who wanted to help me get to the next town could leave an envelope with him before the end of the night, and he would see that I would get it.

It seemed that a few Saints had responded to his announcement. I started with the envelope from the church which held five new one hundred dollar bills, with a note that read, "Brother Vale, God blesses whom he will bless. After you ministered to us last night, of the offering was over $15,000 cash and checks.

We've never seen it this way." And it was signed simply, pastor Marshall.

"Well thank you Lord" I said out loud, "they were due for a good blessing."

"Yes they were." Was the response from the Holy Spirit.

Taking a good mouthful of coffee I decided I'd better get dressed, otherwise I would be there all day. I thought I would make it a jeans and T-shirt day, and dressed accordingly with Levi jeans and a black T-shirt.

As I was returning to the table, there was a knock at the door, and when I opened it found a courier on the other side.

"Vale Thomas?" He asked politely, and at my nod continued saying, "sign here please." Handing me a small clipboard and indicating a line at the bottom. After I had signed it and handed it back to him he passed me an envelope with the Royal Bank of Canada logo at the top left-hand corner.

After he had stepped into the elevator, I closed the door and opened the envelope, which held two things. A letter, and the Visa card which I had applied for several months previously.

The letter read, "Dear Mr. Thomas; it is our good pleasure to inform you that after viewing your application and speaking to your references we have approved your application with a limit of $2000."

There was more written letter including instructions about activating card. That was about all I could take at the moment, and I had to sit down.

I had to go downtown anyways, so I thought I would stop at the bank as I went about my business. Turning my attention to the next envelope which my hand was resting on anyways, I opened it to find a one hundred dollar American bill, a business card from some publishing house in New York, and a hastily hand written note that read as follows:

"God bless you Mr. Thomas. I was in the service last night, and you called for anybody with trouble in their vision. The doctors had told me that without a miracle I would be completely blind in my left eye due to macular degeneration. "

"The minute you said that God wanted to heal everybody with trouble in their eyes, I felt something happen. "

"I thought I had gotten something in my left eye, and so went to the washroom to flush it out. Once I had done that I found that I could see perfectly with both eyes."

That really blessed me, and I was genuinely happy for the man. He went on to say that he was a partner in a publishing house, and that I should call him immediately to set up an interview. There was something else about a book and publications but I had lost all focus as I began to give thanks to God for his goodness.

I started talking to the Lord as I continued to thank him for whatever was or was not happening. "This must be what you meant Lord when you said in your word that you had prepared the work and the work was done suddenly."

"Don't be afraid" was his response.

I took that as an indication the guard was indeed aware of what was happening and all would be well. I began to relax and reached for the next envelope. This one was a little tamer. It was from a widow in the church with $20 and a note that said just a little money for coffee along the way.

The last one was an envelope from the youth group containing $100 and a note that said we are with you, and it was signed by the youth pastor and all 20 of the churches youth group. It all touched my heart so deeply that all I could say was "Lord bless them somehow, and show them your love."

I called the Man from the publishing house that the secretary simply took a message and said he would get back to me.

It was now nearly 2 in the afternoon, and I thought I would go down the street to Houston's pizza for brunch. The meal took about half an hour after which I drove down to the bank and activated my visa card.

When I got home I had just enough time to hang my jacket in the closet and get comfortable in one of the recliners. Then the phone started ringing. I thought at first that it was a series of prank calls.

Some of you might remember being young teenagers, and picking a completely random phone number from the phone book, dialing the number and asking whoever answered, "Hello is your refrigerator running?" And when they answered responding to them by saying, "well you'd better go catch it, it just ran past my place!"

It started with several messages from the local TV stations. Both Global TV as well as CKCK, and then there were the calls from the radio stations. Z99 and CKRM. They were all looking for 'The Miracle Man', and was he available for interviews. Not being sure how to deal with the messages, I erased them all.

I was sure that if it was for real, they would keep calling until they talked to me. I was glad that I had chosen call display when I had the phone service hooked up. The next two calls were from the local papers, followed by a call from Pastor Tony Marshall. I answered that one. "How can I help you Pastor" I asked cheerfully.

"Vale! I'm surprised you're answering your phone, I thought I would have to leave a message" his surprise sounding genuine.

He chuckled when I told him I had call display. "Have you packed for the Dakotas yet?" He continued. When I told him I hadn't he breathed a sigh of relief saying, "I was afraid you'd already left."

I suspected the reason for his call and asked if there had been a change in plan.

"Yes" he said laughing "I was calling to tell you to unpack, and tune your guitar instead." He went on to explain that he had deluged by calls from people around the province, saying they were either driving or flying in, and asking if we would be doing a service tonight. "I've been on the phone since this morning and taken maybe 100 calls from pastors and families.

It sounds like we have between five and 600 people coming for his service tonight. Young man" he said excitedly "it looks like we might be heading into revival!"

As we continued our conversation we both agreed that our storefront church would not accommodate even a fraction of the expected crowd, and Pastor Tony told me that he had booked a conference room at the Sheraton Hotel. He had also shared his excitement with some of the local pastors, and one of them had made some phone calls, and had been able to arrange for a worship team to help us.

Before hanging up, Pastor Tony instructed me to take some of the money the church had given me for travel expenses, and buy a new suit for tonight's' service, and that I should be at the meeting somewhere between 8: 30 and 9 PM. A quick glance at my watch showed me that I had time to get to the Moore's store, which was a block north on Albert Street, just on the right-hand side.

Chapter Two

In my youth and inexperience, I had always gone with the more traditional two piece pinstripe suit. Usually navy blue in color. From tonight on however, it seemed that I was leaving the ministry of helps, and being elevated by the Holy Spirit into the office of the evangelist, and as a result my wardrobe would have to reflect said promotion.

I had been told by many friends that often under the anointing, the color of my eyes changed from green to blue. With that in mind a powder blue suit quickly caught my eye from across the store and the attentive sales team were quick to see that, and quickly ushered me in to the changing room with a pair of matching shoes.

It fit me surprisingly well off the rack, and being on sale I could afford to take two, as well as the shoes and a tie that matched quite well.

Needing only minor alterations, they said they could have both suits ready before closing time. I thanked them and went next door to the Swiss Chalet restaurant for the chicken dinner special.

After getting home with the suits I realize that I needed to get some rest and then pray for the night service. I arrived at the Sheraton at about 8:45 PM, and when Pastor Tony saw me standing at the back of the hall he smiled, gave me two thumbs-up, and a moment later a cordless microphone was brought to me by one of the altar workers. One of the first Nations Pastors from Ocean Man was singing and giving a testimony. When he was done, Pastor Tony gave the signal for me to take the service.

Holding up the microphone, I received a nod from the soundman. I then began to speak softly but clearly about God's love, his mercy and grace.

While I was doing so, the Bible school student from Muskowkwen first Nations made some adjustments to the sound board, and turning up the reverb until I nodded, and I carried on when I was satisfied.

I felt a song welling up in my spirit, got the attention of the worship leader, and told her key of D, and started to sing there's something about that name. Two things happened at that moment. The presence of God filled the hall, and Pastor Tony Jumped to his feet shouting into his mic, "That's an anointing for ten thousand People!"

A wave of reverence to God swept over the crowd, causing those who could to stand and worship with hands raised toward heaven.

When the last verse was sung and the final notes faded into silence there came a murmur of amazement from the section where many men and women in wheel chairs had been brought in.

First, a young boy of thirteen or so, screamed and then went stiff as a board, laughing hysterically as he began to float up above his electric wheelchair. I rebuked the devil and the boy screamed again, and fell to the ground, as limp as a wet dishrag, The next moment he began to praise God as he slowly got his feet under him, and stood to his feet. He took a few shaky steps, praised God, and began to run.

The crowd roared with elation as one by one the wheelchairs emptied and their prior occupants began leaping and dancing and praising God! It was truly a joyous moment, and then people being what they are, it all went bad.

Joy turned to frenzy, and the crowd became a mob that rushed and grabbed hold of me trying to tear or cut away a piece of my clothing or a handful of hair of they could get it.

It all happened so fast that I was helpless and unable to react. The last thing I remember was thinking "and the press is here to get all the action. God help us all". And then all went dark and I could hear the incessant ringing of the telephone. After a moment I realized that it sounded like my telephone.

Opening one eye cautiously, I saw that I was at home, lying on my bed. The phone kept ringing so I got up and answered it, since I saw that it was Pastor Tony. "Hello Pastor" I said cheerfully "you caught me napping, I'm glad you called. There was a chuckle on the other end and I heard the pastor saying, "I thought I might.

The team has already started, and I'm just leaving my house. I wanted to make sure that you were dreaming or watching a movie."

It was my turn to chuckle "no movie Pastor, but you did catch me dreaming. It seemed like God was giving me a wanting or something." The pastor asked me to give him the details of the dream, and after hearing the details, we realized that it would be good to be prepared just in case.

We hung up then and I hurried to get dressed, and got to the Sheraton Hotel at 8:45 PM. We had agreed that I would enter through the back doors and stay there until we saw how things were going to go. Pastor Tony had a team of altar workers waiting for me, who had received orders that if anything should happen their purpose was to get me and the elevator, and over to the Regina inn where I would stay until it was safe for me to go home.

Chapter Three

Everything began to unfold exactly as my dream had gone in detail. I began to sing, Pastor Tony jumped to his feet under the unction of the Holy Ghost shouting, "That's an anointing for 10,000 people!"

Those who could got to their feet and praised God, and at the end of the song a holy hush fell in the place. A young boy of about 13 with what appeared to be multiple sclerosis began to scream and went stiff as a board, then began to levitate. I rebuked the devil and the boy fell to the ground.

A moment later he was on his feet, with no trace of multiple sclerosis, and beginning to walk and praise God, and then all the other wheelchairs began to empty.

It took a moment for the crowd to realize what they had witnessed, and then they jumped to their feet praising God.

Pastor Tony nodded once and the altar workers wisked me out the back door to the elevator and stayed with me until I was safely in a room at the Regina Inn a block away.

The young man had registered me under the name Jesse James, and after they had brought my car over from the Sheraton, they returned to the meeting, and I quickly went home, packed a suitcase, and drove north on Albert Street getting onto the ring road which would take me to Victoria Avenue on the east end of town. Once there I got a few burgers from McDonald's and a large chocolate shake, and afterwards found a nearby 7-11, picked up a few items that I would need for the next few days, and returned to my hotel, parking in the underground lot.

For whatever reason, I had always preferred to watch a movie or some kind of show on TV while I was eating, tonight being no exception.

After finding the remote, it only took a moment to find something suitable, and enjoyed my meal without having to answer the phone or the door.

After the movie it was time for a long hot shower, and I fell asleep and woke up praising God, and thanking him for the heads up. I remember at one point asking God if it would always be that way, and it seemed like he laughed and said, "Yeah, pretty much." Which elicited a chuckle from me.

Later in the afternoon Pastor Tony arrived with his driver and a couple students from Muskowkwen and Pasqua first Nations. The moment they walked in I could see there were all quite pleased with the response that they were getting from around the province.

In our conversation I found out that after I had left things that got out of hand for a minute. When the people realized I had gone, they began to calm down, and they had spent the rest of the evening testifying, worshiping, and of course eating. After the offering and more music and testimony, another collection was taken and a call for pizza sent out.

Pastor Tony talked about many plans for the future and other things, and as he was leaving, suggested that since I was already packed it would be best if I left town for a few weeks in order to give the story enough time to circulate properly.

As I was driving east towards Winnipeg I felt that God had given him wisdom in putting the meetings off for a few weeks in order for excitement and anticipation to build.

For the faith of the people to be properly stirred so that their hearts were ready for anything God wanted to do. Pastor had given me a large brown envelope as he was going out the door saying, "Evangelist, it is safe to say that your ministry is firmly established."

Since I was in no particular hurry I chose to stay at a Super 8 Motel just outside of Portage la Prairie in Manitoba, about an hour west of Winnipeg on the number one highway.

I registered once again under the name Jesse James, and the staff didn't mind so long as the credit card information was correct.

I found that the room was satisfactory, and I went downstairs to the restaurant for a meal. I chose Salisbury steak over the New York, because that's who I was, a man of simple tastes.

Among other things in the envelope that Pastor had given to me, was a rough makeshift itinerary, or in layman's terms, a short list of places and dates that I would visit in the month ahead. At a glance it seemed simple enough. I would spend Thursday, Friday, and Saturday at the healing Centre Church where one of Pastor Tony's drivers would meet me and become my driver for several weeks ahead.

Back in my room, I poured out the contents of the envelope onto the bed. One of the first things I saw was another envelope from the church, and opening it I found a note that said God bless you, along with $5000 in cash.

I immediately put $750 aside as my 15% tithes and offerings. The next envelope that I picked up contained in a check for $1000 and a thank you note from the parents of the boy with MS.

Altogether 37 envelopes and a total of $32,720. In cash and checks, five invitations from local pastors, to more contacts for publishing, and somebody wanting to sell me 23 acres of land with an old church on it for one dollar.

I felt humbled by the gratitude and the generosity of those who had given so generously. The Spirit of the Lord spoke to me at that moment and said, "Look more closely at each gift, and make a record of all of it." What would you do in my case? I obeyed the Lord and immediately went over it again.

The boy name Kyle, born with MS, living with constant pain, and the huge number of pills just to get through each day.

10 others in wheelchairs due to car accidents and spinal injuries who were told they would never walk again for as long as they lived.

Six others had walked into the meeting was extremely large cancer tumors in various parts of their bodies, each of them had walked out of the meeting without the tumors. 15 others crippled by arthritis completely free, and five others with knee injuries completely healed.

When I expressed my wonder and appreciation for all that God had done he responded by saying, "work for me only, and I will build you up and not tear you down."

The following day I drove into Winnipeg and somehow found myself at the Garden City shopping Centre, where I bought my first cell phone, brand-new laptop, a briefcase and a number of journals.

My next stop was the bank where I deposited the cash and checks into my account, keeping a few hundred dollars on me just because.

Chapter Four

The Winnipeg Healing Centre Church was close to the Winnipeg Conference Centre on Portage Avenue. Not at all far from the corner of portage and Main, which is known as the windiest corner in Canada. It took about 45 minutes to find the church and seeing that it would be at least two hours before Pastor Tony and his wife arrived from Regina, I decided to book a room in the adjoining hotel.

The room was fairly large and well appointed, that is to say having all of the amenities. I found everything to my satisfaction, and so turned on the television to find the local news and weather. As happens so often I must've fell asleep during the sports cast, and so missed the weather. Waking up at about 4 PM.

I took a shower and prepared my suit, then called Pastor Tony let him know I was in the hotel and gave him my cell phone number.

He told me that he would be delayed, but that a team should be downstairs to set up the hall and begin the service on time. With that understanding, I went in search of a Boston pizza and was soon and enjoying a big plate of spaghetti and meatballs.

Back in my hotel room I settled in and began to pray for the Christian community, for the healing Centre Church in general, and for the camp meeting. As a rule, I liked to sit before the Lord for about an hour each day, in order to get a sense of God's direction for each day.

In this situation I had a sense of what God wanted to accomplish in this series of meetings.

With that in mind I waited and I prayed until the anticipated knock on the door came, and I was escorted downstairs where I would be given the green light, to obey the Lord.

While I was waiting, the Spirit of the Lord began to talk to me about money. He told me that if there were fewer than 50 people in the membership of the church I was visiting, that I should not receive an offering, but that I should instead leave an offering with them.

I fully agreed with that, and I had faith that of God took me to a small church, he would see to it that I could leave an offering with them. As to the timing of implementing his desire, he simply said begin tonight. And I realized that this was right, as I felt the witness of the Holy Spirit.

A few moments later my phone rang. "Hello Evangelist Thomas" a man's voice said "This is Marcus McDaniels. We haven't met yet, but I did leave my card with your pastor earlier in the week."

I told him I remembered his name and had called to make an appointment. He responded by telling me that this was indeed the purpose for his call. We then began to speak of many things. He advised me that he would be in Winnipeg the following day, and could we meet for lunch? To which I replied in the affirmative.

I asked him if he liked Italian, what he said it was his favorite, I arranged to meet with him at the place where I had eaten earlier. We arrange then to meet at 2 PM, that I should come hungry, and be ready to sign an exclusive contract.

We both laughed then said goodbye, and a moment later the deacon was at the door to accompany me downstairs. By the time we entered the church downstairs, Pastor Tony and his wife had arrived, and the meeting was in full swing.

There were approximately 40 people in the seats when I walked in, and another 10 to 15 people came in after I arrived.

I had been directed to a seat on the platform, and so I waited there for the next 20 minutes or so while Pastor Tony and his wife made announcements and took care of the business of the church. Following which, Pastor Tony's wife, Dorothy Anne Marshall, spoke excitedly about the meetings in Regina.

The miracles which took place on the first night, and how we had so many calls that we had to do extra services the following night and the night after.

She talked also about the Holy Spirit falling like rain, and the hundreds of miracles which had taken place the following night. How the boy with MS had been dramatically delivered from Satan's hand, and that immediately afterwards, 25 more wheelchairs were emptied permanently.

She spoke of how the crowd began to worship at first, and then when it truly sank in what had happened, that the crowd had become a mob at the altar workers barely had time to get me to safety, and that God only knew what might've happened otherwise.

She continued by recounting several miracles that had taken place and reported that every day they were getting more calls concerning miracles that took place on the first night.

She went on to add that the meetings were still going on through worship and testimony in Regina.

She concluded by saying that she believed revival had come to Regina, and used that as a springboard to introducing me, to see what God would do in Winnipeg.

The Holy Spirit impressed upon me that I should start with the hallelujah chorus, and that I should sing it until he told me to sing something different. So I began to sing, working with the dynamics the volume starting strong and melting away to a whisper, and from the whisper to the other end of the scale with a bold and loud voice proclaiming the wonder of God.

When I had everybody on their feet who could stand on their feet, I let them take over the singing. Then when the time was right, I began to exhort them, urging and encouraging them to turn from their sin and turn to God with their whole heart.

I continued until one by one tears welled up in their eyes and they fell to their knees in repentance calling out for God to be merciful.

At this point the Spirit of the living God released me to sing the chorus that we've come to know as 'light the fire in my soul'. And when we had some at through half a dozen times, the fire fell and it was wonderful. Some were laughing, and some were weeping, and others were laughing and weeping. It seemed that no one could stand on their feet, not even to minister.

Even I might as left the sanctuary at that point to let God be God in all things. Finally, after a good long while, the cloud began to dissipate and the people could finally regain their feet. Then one by one they began to move toward the front wanting to testify for what God had done for them.

Retired farmers, their limbs crippled and deformed by arthritis, a few Parkinson's and visible cancer tumors, all set free when the glory cloud fell. With my work done, I went upstairs.

I first indicated my intense to pastor Tony who smiled and gave me the nod indicating he understood and it was fine with him. I tried to be careful not to shake hands or make contact with anyone unless instructed by the Holy Spirit.

On my way upstairs, I began to thank God and to worship in my heart, and in the midst of doing so God spoke to me about many things including the meeting with the publishing house.

"Don't be afraid to accept this offer" he said to me in a still small voice, "I have purposed that because I can trust you with money, you shall prosper in your walk with me."

He went on to tell me that Marcus McDaniel was already talking to people he knew and the recording industry, and they were putting together a record deal for me. I was given the green light to accept that as well. "Others will make you better offers" I was told, "but I have not sent them. " As the elevator reached my floor and I stepped out in the hallway the last thing the Lord said to me even as my stomach began to rumble, was that I was about to have company and that I should order to extra-large all dressed pizzas. I went into my room, and made the call.

A short time later the pizza arrived and was followed closely by Pastor Tony and his wife, and four of the Bible school students from Regina. Well we talked and we ate, and we talked some more.

Chapter Five

It was nearly 2 AM had both
talked and eaten their fill, I cleaned and
straightened up the furniture to the best
of my ability then I lay across my bed
and talked to my father in heaven until I
fell asleep. Pastor Tony's wife had
studied until she was satisfied she knew
and understood the office of the pastor,
and had applied and been accepted for
full ordination.

As was revealed in the
conversation of the night before, Pastor
Dorothy would now shepherd and
oversee the Healing Centre Church in
Regina, while Pastor Tony would now be
known as Bishop Marshall, and would
oversee the Healing Centre Church in
Winnipeg.

Pastor Dorothy would take the morning service, and Bishop Marshall would take the evening service. That left me free to relax and pray some, to relax and prepare for both the business meeting at 2 PM, and more importantly the evening service. I had always liked the expression, "don't put all of your eggs in one basket." And I had liked to believe that God wanted to remind me of one thing with the Ministry.

The one thing that an evangelist or a travelling minister had to understand that from the minute he stepped out the door, it would be chicken one day and feathers the next. Once again, or in other words, it was always feast or famine.

There would be times when the money flowed like water, and they would also be times when there would be barely a trickle of money.

With that in mind I came to understand that there would be times when the ministry would support me, and they would also be times when I would have to support the ministry.

Yes it was sad to say, but at such a time as this the days one a preacher could live of the gospel were long past. I needed therefore, something that would allow me to make money while I slept.

Signing with the book Company would be a good example. What God had said about Marcus McDaniels introducing me to the recording industry would be another.

The more I thought about it the more I realized that videos could very well be another venue, and I purposed in my heart to speak to McDaniels about that. Looking at the time I realized that it was time to dress and go to my meeting with Mr. McDaniels.

I first thought of going with the traditional pinstripe attire, but reconsidered when I saw that I had time to shop for dress casual in the community. With that in mind, I dressed in jeans, T-shirt, and sneakers. Taking my new briefcase with me and making sure I had the key for the room, I headed for the elevator with the front desk as my first stop.

Reaching my first destination, I saw that the hotel staff were courteous and smartly dressed. As I handed them the key for my room and inquired for messages, I also commented on their dress casual attire, asking if they had bought locally.

Two of them weren't sure but the third lady seemed to be just a little sharper than the others, and commented that she did in fact know where the uniforms had been purchased, and that she had been a part of the selection committee.

A moment later she had written the name and address of the store, along with directions on how to get there on foot. I think this the staff for their service, and went in search of what could quickly become my new favourite place to shop.

I found the shop five minutes later, and spent the next half-hour browsing through the store like a kid in a candy shop. Everything looked fabulous! After I had walked through the store in number of times and had viewed the entire inventory, I called upon the sales staff for assistance.

Having made good use of the fitting rooms, it was not long before I had purchased many outfits and returned to my hotel. When I had changed and returned the key to the desk once more, they commented on my new look.

This gave me the opportunity to inquire about a stationary shop along the way to the restaurant, and stocking my briefcase with quality stationary and pens, I carried on to my appointment.

Once inside the restaurant I was asked by the staff if I had a reservation, and I in turn replied by asking if they had a table for McDaniels. I was quickly shown to one of the better tables and the house.

McDaniels and another man were already seated, sipping wine and chatting amiably. Both men stood when I arrived and shook my hand, and then indicated that I should be seated.

I declined the wine that was offered to me, and instead asked for coffee with cream and honey to sweeten it, and I ordered all so water with a twist of lemon.

Marcus began by introducing the other man as a ghost writer named Charlie Malone, and then went on to say that he had taken the liberty of ordering, and he was evidently no stranger to Italian cuisine.

He had ordered several appetizers, various soups, and then several entrées, each is wonderful as the last. We spoke about every aspects of the publishing industry that each of us could think might be even closely related. That is to say I am sure that we exhausted the topic completely.

When it was all said and done the only thing left to talk about was business. I was thankful that Marcus McDaniels had made it easy for me.

Working from what the two of them had already seen and hundreds of testimonies, Charlie Malone had already begun to write what would become my first publication.

Chapter Six

Apparently all that remained was to write about the remainder of this conference and the signs wonders and miracles as they happened, and a proper interview with me. Following that they told me all that remained to be done, apart from my signature on the contract, was for me to proofread approve it and put my name on the cover.

Things were progressing so well McDaniels was saying, and the book so close to going to publication that he and his partners were offering me a check for $10,000 as an incentive for me to join their family of publishers and writers. Keeping in mind what the Holy Spirit had said the night before concerning this, I simply smiled and inquired where I should sign.

After my signatures were properly witnessed, there was more handshaking, many assurances, and then the check was in my hands, and I was officially ushered in to the publishing industry.

As soon as the contracts were brought out, a group of 15 to 20 photographers seem to materialize out of thin air. They captured every signature, every handshake, the presentation of the check and more. I think it was then that I realized there would be a number of promotional interviews and book signings, which would all be a part of a promotional tour to sell the book and me as well.

As we were wrapping up our conversation in getting ready to leave, there was a final flurry of photographs questions and other activity then I was whisked out the door and on my way back to my room.

Along the way, I realized I was walking past the branch of the bank that I dealt with. Remembering the check that I now had in my briefcase I decided to go in and deposit it not leaving anything to chance.

When I got to the teller I put my bank card and the card reader and punched in the code as always. So far so good. I then signed and presented the check to the cashier who asked how much I would like to deposit. When I told her $9,500. She looked at me a little funny, and went to talk to her supervisor who came rushing over.

She asked me to confirm that I wanted to deposit $9500. I confirm that I did indeed want to deposit that amount, at which point she said well I'm afraid then that we will not be able to help you until tomorrow.

I asked her then if there was a problem with the check to which she replied, "No sir everything is fine, we just don't carry that amount of cash."

I was puzzled that this and told her I did not understand. At which point she began to get control of this situation. "You want to deposit $9500 is that correct sir?" When I responded in the affirmative she went on to say, "So then, the check is for $100,000, your deposit would require us to give you $90,000 in cash. I'm sorry sir, we just don't carry a large amount like that at any time." I started to laugh then as I began to understand.

I asked to look at the check and saw that it was a certified cheque in the amount of $100,000. marked advance on royalties, and signed by two officials of the publishing house.

"I see the error," of my words. I told her still laughing "I thought the check was for $10,000. I was only wanting to take $500 home with me. Please allow me to increase the amount of the deposit to $99,500."

At this she visibly brightened and began to chuckle herself, and then asked what it was all about. I told her about signing with the publishing house and was under the impression they were giving me a signing bonus of $10,000. I certainly had no idea that they were giving me a check for much more.

On a whim I decided to look through the contract papers and sure enough, there was another check mixed in with the papers for $10,000. I smiled and handed the check to the teller indicating that I would like to also deposit that check. She just smiled and asked for my signature and everything was done quickly. I knew that God had truly set this whole thing in motion.

When the teller asked if there was anything else I'd like to do, I replied that there was, and a short time later left the bank with a certified cheque for $5000 for the healing center church.

This had very little to do with paying tithes, and everything to do with the covenant which God had established with me just a short time ago.

I had felt the witness of the Holy Spirit the very moment that I asked for the certified cheque. Back in my hotel room, I saw that I had a few hours left before they would be calling for me in the service. There are times in the lives of men and women when God does things for us and we give him a heartfelt thank you, and very little else. For the most part that seems to be fine.

On the other side of the coin there are times that God does things for us and a heartfelt thank you is nowhere near enough.

Chapter Seven

This was one of those times. I sat on the bed and I talked to God for over an hour. At first he seemed not to hear. It's interesting. When God pretends not to listen, it shows that he has something in mind, and is somehow testing our hearts.

Because I was persistent, it pleased the Lord to answer my questions. I felt it was important for me to understand why he had opened this window of opportunity for me.

"Your word clearly states Lord that those who preach the gospel should live of the gospel."

He responded by saying "Go on."

"You also say in your word that the just shall live by faith."

"Yes that's true." He said, "Son, I see the confusion of your heart. I also said that obedience brings the blessing. Moreover" he continued, "I also said beloved, I would above all things that you should prosper and be in health, even as your soul prospers."

It was my turn now to respond by saying, "yes, that's true. But still Lord, did not the apostle Paul teach that we should not teach the gospel for filthy lucre?"

The Spirit of the Lord responded yet again by saying, "remember that I will bless whom I will bless."

"Thank you father" I replied "I needed to be sure."

"Understand this my son. If you were poor and unknown, I would not be able to use you in the way that I desire."

"For that reason if I bless you and make your name great I can use you to a far greater measure. Be not afraid son, but let me bless you."

"Yes Lord I see that, thank you for it. Just one more question if I may Lord?"

"Certainly my son." Came the reply.

I smiled and then asked, "Lord, why did you hesitate to answer?"

He hesitated for another moment and then answered by saying, "I wanted to see if you would wait for my answer, or if you would make assumptions. "

I closed the conversation by saying simply, "thank you."

Checking the time, I saw that I still had the luxury of a power nap, and a closing my eyes I took full advantage of the opportunity.

I don't know how long I had been sleeping, but suddenly I found myself walking under a clear blue sky and surrounded by a sea of golden wheat ready harvest.

I could not remember when the dream had begun, but it was always the same. The sky, the sea of wheat, the laughter of children, bird song in the distance. Then without warning, a blinding flash of light stretching across the horizon, and then it was all gone.

The sea of wheat crushed and burnt. Mothers weeping for their children. Broken and wounded people everywhere, and the unbearable sounds of human suffering. Crying for God to be merciful and heal their wounds. The Voice of the Lord speaking to me saying, "My son, go and heal my people."

This time however, the sound of a telephone ringing somewhere began to draw me up and out of the dream."

It was Bishop Marshal, telling me that the meeting had been moved to a larger hall, because many of the local pastors had somehow heard of what God was doing, and wanted to bring their people to be a part of it.

When I asked for a guess-timation there was a pause on his end, and then he simply said that it would be our largest crowd ever.

I had a quick snack of juice, grapes, and cheese, in an effort to keep my energy levels balanced. A little something I had learned in Music College, a tip from one of the teachers which had served me well on several occasions.

Looking over my woefully limited wardrobe, I chose the blue ensemble from Moore's. I was particularly pleased with the vast that had come with the suit. I suppose I have always had a thing for a good vast.

The double-breasted jacket with the shiny buttons fit better than I remembered when I tried it on, and I had to admit as I examined it in the mirror that it made me look good, and looking good meant that I could be confident.

One last look in the mirror was all I had time for, as the familiar knock on the door by the deacons sent to drive me, meant that it was ShowTime.

Handing my key to Deacon Walker, I waited while he handed it to the staff member behind the counter and they came and opened the door for me and we stepped out into the evening. Parked in front of the doors was Bishop Marshal's shiny new Lincoln town car.

The deacon opened the back door allowing me to slide into the back seat and closed it once I was seated, and walked around to the driver seat.

Once he was seated behind the wheel, I asked if we were waiting for Bishop Marshal, to which he replied in the negative and pulled away from the curb. Once we were underway I pulled an envelope from the inside pocket of my jacket and waited for him to stop at the first red light, and then handed it to him saying, "A little coffee money Deacon Walker." He thanked me for it and continued driving as the light turned green.

A short time later we pulled up at a side entrance of a concert venue that would seat approximately 5000 people. From the cars and buses that I could see in the parking lot I realize that it must very nearly be already filled. As the deacon was showing me to a room where I would wait and prepare, I could hear the worship team playing some of Bishop Marshal's standards.

While I was receiving God's instructions for my part in the service, I was told to start by calling out a few specific people and conditions, and that the rest depended on the response of the crowd, indicating that I should mark and stay close to one of the many exits.

Being somewhat impressed with the comfort of the town car, I was glad that I had sent my 65 Impala to the shop for a complete overhaul. I had previously mentioned to pass to Tony that I was getting my car rebuilt and asked him if he knew of someone who needed a blessing.

He had responded by saying that yes he knew of a young family on ocean man reserve who would be happy to have it. We had finished the paperwork and I handed him the keys before the pizza was finished the previous night.

Chapter Eight

That was how he trained his Bible students. But when you upgraded to a new vehicle or a new house, he did not sell the old one or treated in, you fixed it so that he could be a blessing to another child of God, and so the Impala was being restored from bumper-to-bumper.

Clearing my mind of all distractions, I began to pray in tongues until it was time, and the time came soon enough. 45 minutes later the last of the Pastors had been recognized, and given an opportunity to speak briefly about his or her church. It was then time for Pastor Dorothy to conduct the business of the ministry.

One of the deacons finally came to escort me into the service, and as we walked I went through the mental list that I had made of everything I had been instructed to do.

The place was larger on the inside than it looked on the outside, and I was glad that one of the deacons at least was familiar with the layout of the building.

Once inside the main arena I saw that most of the seats were filled, and had begun to imagine that a hold the size would have an overflow section that could hold another 200 to 300 people. The door through which we had entered, was just to the left of the platform area, and a cordless microphone was brought to me as I reach the top of the three short steps.

I began by speaking slowly and naturally, giving the sound person time to adjust the microphone to my voice. What he looked at me I was not quite satisfied with the sound and asked him to add some reverb to add some warmth to my voice.

"Hallelujah to the Lamb" I began "we are on the holy ground. We are meeting on holy ground, for I feel the Lord is here in this place, and where he is, is holy ground."

"Can I get some reverb on the microphone? Yes that's better. Just a little more please, that's perfect hold it right there." I began to sing a holy ground because when I began to talk about the Lord's presence in the building, I felt off all the harsh sweep through the place.

By the time we started the second verse the people were already weeping. Some falling to their knees weeping before the Lord. In a matter of just a few short minutes, the altar area in front of the platform was filled with penitent sinners, and hundreds of seats were empty.

Chapter Nine

I continued to sing, pausing just long enough to ask the pastors to come and lead the people in prayers of repentance.

By the time the pastors had reached the altar, I was into the second song. "There is a river that flows from deep within, there is a river that cleanses from all sin. Come to the water there is a vast supply, come to the river it never shall run dry."

By the time I had sung this him through for the third time the pastors had prayed, and the people were ready to return to their seats. We sang it one more time, and then I called for all of those who had felt the touch of God in areas where they had been afflicted, to come forward. I now called for the altar workers of the healing center church to come and check the people.

They would ask where the pain was and if it was still there. They would also ask what God had done.

Those who said that God had just touched them wonderfully, and they were filled with peace, were led to one side where a deacon would pray with them.

Those who said "the pain was here or there and now it's gone!" Were led up onto the platform, where they testified and were quickly led from the platform, and allowed to return to their seats.

Some spoke of back pain, others of headaches, and still others of incurable pain in various parts of the body. All of them declared that they were now pain-free and demonstrated by moving in ways that they had not been able to move for a very long time.

It took about 20 minutes to go through the line, and when it was done I began to praise the Lord for his miracles and healing touch.

"But I thank you for all those who came forward, but there are still some who you said would be healed, that we have not yet seen."

"There is one here with a back brace. You were in a car wreck six months ago, and you were told by the doctors you would only need to brace for six weeks." I looked over to my right, and began to suit to point to the third row saying, "You're over here to my right wearing blue and red."

I stopped pointing when I saw a middle-aged woman wearing blue and red sitting in her chair, caught up in the spirit and oblivious to all that was happening around her.

Sending an altar worker to bring her down, I quickly moved on and called for someone who had injured a knee three weeks past, and it was still hurting. "God is touching you right now!" I said loudly.

As I began to look to my left, to see if the individual was over in that section, there was a loud crash from the first balcony, and Bishop Marshall was on his microphone speaking in a commanding tone, "Somebody get there!" And a moment later a young man from the Bible school was with one of the cameramen who was feeling the power of God, moving backwards and trying desperately to stay on his feet.

He had already plowed through two rows of chairs, and by the time he crashed through the third row, he lost the battle and was assisted gently to the floor by the younger altar worker. If anyone had been getting bored, or ready to fall asleep, everybody was now fully alert and laughing softly.

The camera man was back on his feet a few moments later and I motioned for him to be brought down to the platform.

The woman with the back brace had now reached the platform accompanied by another woman who was later identified as her doctor.

I began to speak first to the woman saying, "You weren't going to come tonight were you?"

She began to shake her head vehemently saying, "I certainly did not want to come here tonight. Until you began to sing I thought this was all a bunch of phony baloney, and that your religion had nothing to do with God! "

I had to chuckle and asked her, "and do you still feel that way?"

"I don't know what I feel now!" She responded, "I was just minding my own business" she continued, "and when you started to sing, I felt burning heat shoot through my spine, and it still feels like fire!"

"And who is this with you?" I asked her.

She responded by saying, "this is Dr. Jackson, my back specialist." I then began to talk with the specialist, asking about the particulars of the injury, after which I asked if she would remove the back brace and examine her patient on the spot. At that point she spoke of a colleague who was also in the auditorium, and asked if he could come and assist her in the examination.

I welcomed the opportunity to have two doctors examine this woman and so indicated that the doctor should be found and brought forward.

Chapter Ten

A few moments later both doctors had   gently removed the back brace, touching and prodding, asking the woman to first twist from side to side, and then to bend over and touch her toes when she did with ease. Both doctors through their hands up and said, "She doesn't need this!" Holding up the brace.

This elicited a standing ovation of thunderous applause and praise for the Lord from the crowd, which went on for several minutes. In the midst of it Bishop Marshall caught my attention and with a nod of his head, indicated that he would take over from there. Returning his nod I smiled, handed the mic to one of the altar workers, walked off the platform and was met once more by Deacon Walker who was my chauffeur back to the hotel.

Once inside the hotel I collected my key from the desk clerk, inquired for messages and went up to my room. I quickly changed into comfortable attire and found a movie to watch. Seeing that the movie would not start for half an hour I turned it to the news, and turned down the volume as I began to relax I thank God for everything he was doing and then realized I was really too tired to talk to anyone, and opted for a nice hot shower.

I must've fallen asleep shortly after the movie began and I slept soundly, waking up around 10 AM. I dressed casually and went to have breakfast downstairs eggs bacon hash browns and toast served with a bottomless cup of coffee.

Having played my part in the healing center meetings, and no plans for the next few days, I decided to keep the room for a few extra days and just rest.

That turned out to be a good decision. Soon after I got back to my room phone started to ring. The first call was from Bishop Marshall, who said he wanted to meet in the hotel restaurant in half an hour, which would put it right around 12 noon.

The next call was from McDaniels, who among other things said that he wanted me in New York two weeks from today to release my first book. I asked him to send me an email with the necessary information.

Several minutes later I had the requested information along with an itinerary of appearances and book signings for the next six months. Soon after that conversation, there was a call from Montgomery Jackson, who was in the hotel lobby, and could I meet him downstairs pronto. Without even thinking I found myself agreeing to his request, and was on my way to the elevator.

Five minutes later I was shaking hands with them in the lobby, where he declined my offer for coffee and got straight to the point.

He began by saying, him "I got your number from McDaniels last night, I was here with my boy. The doctors had given him six months to live, cancer of the stomach, and a large tumor on the brain. When you came in last night and started to sing, my son doubled over like he'd been gut shot." He paused here for a moment like he was afraid if he said it too loud it would all be untrue.

"Well" he continued, "my son needed to get to the men's room, so I helped him get there. When I asked him if he was all right, he said he was burnin'up. From head to foot, he said everything was burning. Then he went in the toilet and threw something up, and when he came out of the stall I guess I couldn't stop staring."

I could see the relief in his face, and I was afraid he would start to weep right there in the lobby. I started looking for a tissue box, but then he was speaking again.

"After a time" he said "my son got irritated and asked what I was looking at. All I could do was tell him was to look in the mirror and you'll see. The brain Tumor was gone, and the swelling in his stomach was gone too.

Well we flew our doctors in from the States, and they checked him out after we left the service.

He's cancer free! Got told me to give you this and not say anything else, so God bless you and thank you for obeying the Lord!"

I took the envelope that he put in my hands, and before I could say thank you, all I could see was his back as he vanished through the door.

Back in my room, I asked God about the contents of the envelope before I opened it.

"Don't worry son" he told me, "it is for your personal use. Put your tithes and offerings in a separate account, and I will show you when and where to use it."

I didn't look to see what was inside. I simply placed the envelope in my briefcase and simply gave thanks with a grateful heart. When I looked at my watch again, it was time to meet Bishop Marshall.

He was already seated when I arrived, and as there was only one seat left open, I understood that it was mine, and sat down directly across from him. We talked about the events of the past few weeks, and how quickly God was moving.

He thanked me for my offering, and handed me a package of envelopes with my name on them. "If you ever feel the need for ordination Brother Vale, you will have my support." I thanked him, and he stood up and left with his entourage of deacons and bible students.

As I was paying the bill at the restaurant, my phone began to ring again. It was McDaniels informing me that he had set up a recording deal for me and could I be in New York a week early? I told him I thought I could manage it, and we let it go at that.

Chapter Eleven

While enroute to my room I began to think about how to manage the rest of my day. By the time I unlocked my door, I had set a few priorities. Beginning with the envelopes from the previous night. The first envelope that I pulled out of the briefcase was Mr. Jackson's.

Inside I found three things. First there was the deed to a property in Austin Texas including a photo of a beautiful church building and parking lot. The second thing I found was a note hastily scrawled, saying that his lawyer would be at the hotel at 1 PM this afternoon to take care of the legal matters. The icing on the cake was a certified cheque for $2.5 million US funds. As I held the check and looked at it all I could think to say was, "Lord thank you for this, and thank you for Montgomery Jackson."

The majority of the remaining envelopes were from various places in Manitoba and Saskatchewan, and even a few from Ontario, containing various amounts from 20 to 100 dollars. The others contained letters of thanks, and invitations to do house meetings.

As I began to wonder if I should respond to any of these invitations, I was rescued by the ringing of the house phone, which proved to be Jackson's lawyers who said they would meet me in the restaurant. Another trip downstairs, another coffee with a light snack, and more greetings and handshaking.

Once we were seated and refreshments ordered it was down to business. Signatures were quickly dispensed with, duly witnessed, the title and property officially transferred to my name.

The building itself was less than five years old, and came fully furnished. The main sanctuary seated 5000 people comfortably with a spacious and beautiful platform and amp or altar area security system, PA system, instruments, and more. It was situated on a 25 acre lot, which meant there was room to expand at need.

The basement was home to a Bible college with many classrooms and several offices, and included an auditorium which would accommodate 2000 students and faculty. When I asked why such a beautiful building was on the market so quickly after being built, I was told that the pastor and his wife and three children had died suddenly in a car wreck, and the people had all moved away.

It was really quite tragic, the family had been writing it all in one car and had God's caught in the middle of a multicar pileup which had involved over 100 vehicles. 30 people had been sent to hospital with life threatening injuries and the pastor and his family were not among those who survived.

They had been travelling on the freeway to view the brand-new homes which had been built for the pastor and each of his children when tragedy struck. The four houses had been tied to the church property, and so they also were signed over to me

I was then told that Montgomery Jackson was a real estate mogul who dealt mostly in high profile properties, which is how he came into possession of the church which had just been handed to me.

At this point in the conversation I was handed a set of keys along with the paperwork and titles and deeds, and told that I could take immediate possession.

With the business out of the way as if on cue, the refreshments arrived and the conversation turned from business to pleasure and sports, chiefly baseball and football. The team of lawyers left soon after, leaving me time for two very important chores, the business at the bank and then shopping.

At the bank I made the deposits and set up the tithe account, which meant transferring the appropriate funds, and also increasing the limit on my credit card. With that done I had the bank manager call me a taxi, and went shopping for a new vehicle.

Being still a young man, in my early 30s, I had the initial inclination to shop first for a new Lamborghini or Maserati. The Holy Spirit quickly prevailed, sending me to the largest Ford dealership in Winnipeg where I purchased a forest green fully loaded Lincoln Continental. It seemed that my father had an image for me to uphold.

I don't believe that there is anyone alive who does not love that new car smell, but with my new Lincoln insured and topped up with gas, it was time to enter the long and McQuoid music store into the GPS and complete my shopping for the day.

For a new guitar I had chosen a white Gretsch Panther center- Block and a Marshal 100 watt amplifier to power it, as well as a Zoom G5N pedal for effects. The last stop before going back to my hotel was of course the Italian restaurant.

Whether it was the service or the food or both, really didn't matter. I just enjoyed eating there. While I was enjoying my dinner, I realized there with the changes to my schedule, I would have to leave tomorrow.

For whatever reason, I had slept like a log. In other words, as soon as my head hit the pillow I slept soundly until almost checkout time.

I was glad that I had asked for a wake-up call when I picked up my key at the desk. The shower and shave followed by fresh casual clothes.

A breakfast of sausage and eggs bacon and toast and a generous supply of coffee, and I was ready to check out. My Continental was nice to drive in the city, but on the highway it was an absolute dream. The ride was smooth and quiet and the stereo was wonderfully mellow.

Chapter Twelve

Arriving in Regina around 8 PM I stopped long enough to pick up a bucket of Kentucky fried chicken with fries and gravy and macaroni salad, which included a 2 L bottle of Pepsi. Supplied with hot food, I was ready for a good movie, followed soon after by a sleep in my own bed.

I watched dances with wolves with Kevin Costner, because it always made it easy to fall asleep afterwards, and I was not disappointed.

Waking up around 10 AM I made a simple breakfast. Poached eggs, toast, and two links of sausage, and coffee. Following breakfast I drove to the nearest SGI office and had my Continental properly plated and insured.

It was a good feeling to pay for the four years insurance all at once, and even the license issuer seemed to look at me with a new respect. I then went home after picking up a few groceries.

Bread, milk, eggs and then spent the rest of the day getting acquainted with my new sound.

In so doing, I had time to think. New York was at least five days drive, maybe six or seven for me because I liked to stop and rest every now and then. I realized if I flew I could be there in one day, and have time to explore the city at least in part.

With that in mind, I made the call to Regina International, and made arrangements to fly out on Wednesday morning.

In preparation for my trip, not knowing how long I would be gone, I gave my landlord postdated cheques to cover the rent for the next three months, I had also arranged with him to put my mail under the door.

Just as a precaution. The Continental was my next priority. I decided to park in my underground parking space, and made use of the cover that they had given me as part of a purchasing bonus in Winnipeg. Having slept soundly through the night, I woke up fully refreshed on Wednesday morning.

After a leisurely breakfast I checked my suitcase one last time following the checklist I had prepared, and as I said it by the door of my apartment, thought of my passport. "The passports are important." I told myself, and retreated from my bedroom where it might've stayed.

Though I used my Canadian passport primarily I always carried the American passport with me also. I had grown up in Canada, but had not known that my mother was an American citizen until recently.

Satisfied that I had done all I could do, I set the deadbolt and went downstairs to meet the taxi. Regina International Airport was not large by any stretch of the imagination, and so it took no time at all to get to my gate.

The only time I had ever flown previously was when I had been splitting cedar in the bush on Vancouver Island, and the boss had asked the helicopter pilot to fly us back to camp.

This then would be my first real flight and I was glad I had booked first class. While I was waiting I received a message from McDaniel's personal secretary, that he would meet me at JFK.

While I was waiting for my boarding call, I decided to start reading the copy of the New York Times that I had purchased while walking through Regina International.

I was about halfway through it when I heard the first boarding call for first-class, and when I looked up and saw the stewardesses looking at me questioningly, I realized, "that's for me!" and I hurried to find my seat. Placing my briefcase in the overhead compartment, I settled into my seat to finish reading the Times.

When I realized we were beginning to taxi toward our runway I felt a heightened sense of anxiousness, and took a few deep breaths as I looked out the window. After the 747 had made a turn or two we seem to stand still for a moment. I then heard the engines accelerating as we began to move forward again picking up speed for takeoff.

Once in the air I felt the anxiety return along with a shortness of breath, and I began to wonder about that.

My question was answered as we began to level off. An elderly lady in the aisle next to me was clutching her chest, and she had signaled for the stewardess. Her face had gone ashen grey and her lips were turning from purple to blue, and I knew from my first aid training that she was having a heart attack.

As the stewardess reached her I began to pray saying, "help that Lord!" To which he quickly responded to by saying, "that's why you're here." Understanding that he was telling me to minister to her, I unbuckled my seat belt and went to help the stewardess who was now looking at me.

She gave me room as I reached the distressed passenger, and not knowing what else to do, I put a hand on her shoulder saying, "not on my watch devil, turned her loose!" She immediately began to breathe easier, and the colour came back to her face.

Putting her hand on top of mine she smiled as she took another deep breath and getting stronger by the moment saying, thank you Mr. Thomas."

Returning her smile I went back to my seat and buckled in again as the stewardess checked on her condition again, and being satisfied, return to her duties. The remainder of the flight proved to be uneventful. Rose Baxter, the lady from across the aisle came over and sat next to me for a while, and we had a wonderful conversation. Her husband Jonathan, was the head of a large organization. She was on her way to speak at a women's conference in New York.

When I told her that I was on my way to my first book release, she smiled and said, "Yes I know. They have your picture in every bookstore in New York advertising that event."

"Do they really?" I asked laughing, "I guess that means I need a disguise." We both laughed about that and talked until the juice cart came down the aisle and she went back to her seat. When we landed at JFK, they tried to bring a wheelchair for Rose who firmly rejected the offer saying, "I haven't felt this good for years!" And insisted and walking off the plane unassisted.

I had to chuckle as I thank God for what it done for Rose collected my belongings from the overhead compartment, and went to embark upon the adventure of finding McDaniel's.

Chapter Thirteen

The differences between JFK and Regina International were like night and day. Regina International was small and quiet, and one might go so far as to say that it was orderly. JFK was very large and very busy.

As I began to wonder how to find the arrival gates I heard a commotion behind me. Turning, toward the sound I saw a Rose Baxter speeding towards me driving a golf cart which she had clearly commandeered from the security guard in the seat beside her.

"Come aboard Mr. Thomas!" She commanded, and as I complied she went speeding through the crowd, laughing and shouting, and tooting the horn, "This young man came to take me to see the EMTs", she told me. They want to give me an EEG! I hope they don't give me a breathalyzer!"

She soon got me where I was going, and then sped off again with the security guard beside her barely able to contain his laughter. Collecting my suitcase from the carousel I went in search of what I hoped would be a more sober ride.

I turned on my cell phone in an effort to find my needle in a haystack, but before I could dial McDaniels, I heard my name broadcast over the PA system with a set location to meet my party. This made it easy to get directions, and it did not take long at all to get there.

McDaniels turned out to be a middle aged man, about five foot ten inches tall, slim and well groomed. Wearing tan slacks and a very loud Hawaiian shirt, I might have walked past him had he not been holding a sign with my name on it. "McDaniels?" I asked, as I let go of my suitcase and extended my hand towards him.

"That's right mister Thomas, Marcus McDaniels. How was your flight?"

"It was fine I suppose" I went first class, and this was my first flight."

"Glad to hear it!" he responded cheerfully, "Let's get you to the hotel first, and then we can think about a proper meal for you." There was a stretch limo waiting for us at the curb in front of the terminal.

The driver was dark skinned with dreadlocks peeking out from under his chauffer's cap, he introduced himself as Winston and he spoke with the bit of a Jamaican accent.

With the two of us seated in the back and the driver behind the wheel, we pulled away from the curb and into the flow of traffic.

Our conversation was casual in nature and after a few moments Marcus commented that the restaurant would be closed by the time we got there and asked if I had any preference for take-out. I began to feel that jet leg catching up with me and could think of only one thing, which was a fully loaded pizza and Pepsi.

I must've fallen asleep during all well in our conversation, because when I woke up we were just pulling up in front of the grand Hotel in what Marcus had called the SoHo district. We had apparently stopped and picked up a pizza and so I knew I had been out for quite some time.

The registration was quick and easy. To my surprise and delight, my room was the grand suite on the 16th floor.

McDaniels took care of the tip for the bellhop, made sure that everything was in order, and said he would call in the morning and not to open the door for anyone. Once he was gone, I set the deadbolt and the safety latch, found the remote and turned on the plasma TV.

I then showered and dressed in PJs, found an old John Wayne movie, gave thanks for the pizza, and watched the movie.

As I watched the show I began to talk to God about his goodness and his steadfast love. I suppose it was in reality just to express gratitude and appreciation. It was heartfelt, and never seemed to be really adequate.

I prayed that he would be sovereign in all things that lay ahead, because I had no idea what to expect. At which point he interjected that I should not be worried and just trust him in all things, He would look after me.

Chapter Fourteen

I must've fallen asleep soon after, which often happened for some reason. I had indeed fallen asleep on the sofa, the pizza still on the coffee table and the movie was long finished.

I prayed for God's protection and seeing that it was just after 6 AM, made my way to the master bedroom, and fell asleep in the king-size bed where I slept until the ringing of the telephone woke me hours later. It was Marcus of course, asking if the room was to my liking.

He began to give me a rundown of what to expect through the course of the day, Saying that he did not see a guitar with me, and that we should perhaps start the day browsing through some of the music stores of SoHo.

He said that I should get something to eat downstairs, and that he would pick me up in about three hours. He also gave me the combination to the private safe which he had received from the bellhop, and suggested that I place any valuables in its while I was out of the room.

I say goodbye and followed his suggestion, and took only my wallet with me. New York was after all, New York. I found the restaurant to my liking, ordered the steak and Benedict, was given a complimentary copy of the Times, and enjoyed a leisurely brunch.

The Holy Spirit began to talk to me while I was enjoying my breakfast. He told me that I would be put to the test sometime in the afternoon, and that I should simply say no to whatever they put in front of me. I was on my 3rd cup of coffee when I finished the times, paid my bill, and went back upstairs where I waited for Marcus.

The test came as I got in the elevator to go back to my room. A group of men and women followed me into the elevator and pushed the button for the fourth floor. They asked where I was going and I told them I was going to the seventh floor, and one of the young ladies pushed the button for me. One of them then showed me a syringe and a handful of pills. Another one showed me a bag of white powder and still another showed me a bag of marijuana. I held up one hand as I looked at them all and said, "Thank you no."

Everything disappeared in the blink of an eye, the elevator opened on to the fourth floor and they were gone. I then pushed the button for the 16th floor, and went up to my room to pray for them. I actually prayed for them as I rode up in the elevator.

Back in my suite, I found all the elements necessary to make a pot of coffee, including bottled water, and then sat quietly before the Lord, enjoying the quietness and serenity of the room. More than anything else I believe this to be my most enjoyable part of each day.

It was a not a time of meditation or of any kind. Nor was it a time of being one with the universe. It was not even a time of emptying oneself for the purpose of achieving nothingness. It was not a time of prayer nor praise, neither was it a time of talking to him that he is and was and is to come.

It was simply a time of quieting the soul, stilling the self-talk, and sitting quietly in the presence of the Lord. Here in this place, the material world faded into obscurity, and the kingdom of heaven became tangible.

A man could spend hours in this place, and feel that he had been there for just a few short minutes.

The ringing of my cell phone brought me back to the live a day world, and as expected, Marcus was waiting for me downstairs.

Making sure the door was securely locked and latched, I made my way to the elevator and then to the lobby. The predominance of gold and marble in the lobby or a subtle hint of the opulence and reality of the American dream.

Surrounded by the soft hues, it would be nothing to settle comfortably into the soft leather furnishings and dream of prosperity. That dream however was for another day.

Ignoring the comfort and opulence, I made my way to the exit and out onto the busy street where my next adventure was beginning.

Once outside, I found the limo part by the curb and Winston standing by the back door, which he opened as I approached. After exchanging hellos as a courtesy, and being safely ensconced in the backseat, the door was closed and seconds later, Winston was back behind the wheel.

Being alone in the backseat I asked my driver where McDaniels was, and I was told that he was waiting for me at the music store. I settled back in the soft patent leather upholstery and enjoyed the ride. After 10 minutes I located the button for the intercom to get my driver's attention. "Yo Winston" I began, "

"Yes sir?" He replied with a smile.

I called him my brother and asked, "why do I get the feeling were not in Kansas anymore?"

My driver laughed and by replied saying, "change of plan Mr. Thomas, we will be meeting Mr. Marcus soon."

Before I could ask another question the Holy Spirit was speaking to me saying, "Son, his mother is dying of cancer, his wife needs a kidney transplant, and his son has a terminal brain tumor. He's hoping you will go and heal them all."

"What should I do?" I asked hesitantly.

"Tell him not to worry, but to turn around and take you to your meeting. I have healed them because of his faith. In a few minutes he will get a phone call confirming this."

I pushed the button on the intercom again, and when he answered I said calmly "Winston, God has seen your Faith, and the suffering of your family. He has seen the anguish of your soul, and healed them all.

Turn us around brother and take me shopping, and as you do you will get a phone call confirming these things."

As he looked quickly into the rearview mirror eyes wide with surprise and filled with tears, he nodded his thanks and turned around at the first opportunity.

A moment later I saw him on the phone, and his smile told me all I need to know. We pulled up to the music store 20 minutes late, and I explained to McDaniels that I had to go back and get my wallet.

Chapter Fifteen

Seeming to accept that, Marcus then introduced me to the manager of the store, Judy's Music on Broome Street in the SoHo District, explaining that I needed to find some equipment quickly to do some recording.

The manager then asked me a few questions, which guitars I had played, who my guitar heroes were, and what kind of sound I was looking to make. I started by telling him I liked the sounds of the 60s bands.

I told him also that I was looking for something that would give me a clean sound, but allow me to throw in some attitude at will. I said also that I like the Irish delay of the band U2.

That I wanted something also which would allow me to record rhythm loops, allowing me to practice scales and phrases over top of them.

An amplifier small enough to use in my hotel room, but big enough to play a good-sized hall. "I know I'm not asking for much" I said with a grin, "but I'm a man of simple tastes. "

The manager (whose name was James) seemed to understand and appreciate the humor, and replied by saying "let's see what we have laying around."

He then led us through the store section by section, and began to suggest and demonstrate various pieces of equipment.

Beginning with the Boss G 10 with its various presets and looping features, and a zoom G5N, which was very similar to the boss pedal but more compact and lighter.

He also suggested the boss VE 20 focal processor which would get me started, and also had a looping feature on it as well.

He then showed me various guitars. Ibanez, Washburn, Pantera, Gibson, Peavy, the whole range including the Ovation and the Takamine G2. In the end, I decided on three guitars. From the 60s era, I chose a Fender Stratocaster which was rumoured they said to them played by Jimmy. From the 70s era, I chose a Gibson Les Paul. And from the late 50s era of Fender telecaster

For amplification, in view of the guitars that I had chosen they suggested first the Marshall half stack with the 50 watt head. Large enough for any hall but too big to pack around in a rental car, or a hotel room. They showed me Vox, Orange, Fender, but in the end I went with a more compact Marshall 50 Watt amplifier. More compact and still a great range of sound.

I took a vocal processor simply because it was a new toy. I couldn't decide which effects pedal I like better, so I took them both.

And then there were various and sundry accessories such as guitar picks, straps and stands, protective cases that could stand up to being run over by a Mack truck. Metal slides, ceramic slides, a WA pedal, and just because it seemed like a good idea at the time, I even let them talk me into buying a Tascam 36 home recording unit. This meant microphones, cables, a couple good sets of headphones, and oh yes, a York PA system to top it all off.

An hour later we had packed everything upstairs to my hotel suite. We had stopped on the way back to the hotel to ensure everything, and so as long as we made sure that the locks were locked when we left it was all covered.

We had moved it into the hotel, but I would set it up over the next few days, and then become acquainted with it all. I was so happy to get all of this equipment, that I had promised that I would buy them supper.

In the end in the interest of saving time, we went down to the hotel restaurant. A richly appointed place with a pleasant ambience.

Winston ordered the seafood medley with lobster salmon scallops and shrimp served on a bed of rice, and clam chowder as an appetizer.

Marcus ordered New York steak and lobster with baked potato sour cream and chives and he also took the clam chowder for the appetizer. For myself I took a 16 ounce steak and I had been wanting lasagna for days. I went with the Caesar's for the starter.

Instead of wine or coffee I asked for water with a lemon wedge, and the others followed suit. The restaurant had a good reputation and it did not disappoint.

The service was good food was excellent and cooked to perfection and the staff was courteous and attentive.

It was rather pleasant to have company with a meal for a change, and I enjoyed every moment of the conversation.

As much as we would have enjoyed turning on a football game and grabbing a power nap it was time for business and back in my room I didn't even look to see which guitar was taking.

I just grabbed the nearest case, a couple of cables, the G5 pedal, and was back downstairs were the guys were waiting, in just a few minutes.

I had left the amplifier behind because Marcus had said I wouldn't need it.

As it turned out, I got my power nap inadvertently en route to the studio, and I suspect that McDaniels had done the same.

The sign on the building simply read "Caveman Productions", and sported a cartoon picture of a long-haired man dressed in animal skins and sandals, carrying a flying the guitar over one shoulder, in place of the traditional club.

Marcus made a quick call as he got out of the limo, and we were met at the desk by a well-dressed receptionist who recognized Marcus and ushered us into the manager's office without hesitation.

Chapter Sixteen

From the manner of their conversation, it seemed that they were old friends, chatting amiably for several minutes before introductions were made.

"Chris Chatterton, Vale Thomas" Marcus said as he handled the introductions, "Vale Thomas, Chris Chatterton." We shook hands in a businesslike manner along with formal greetings. With that out of the way I commented on his sign saying "I saw you sign on the way in, very nice, very nice. I like your man's choice of axe."

Chris smiled his response saying "thank you, thank you very much". Marcus went on to say that Chris was the music director for one of the larger churches in the district, and that he worked with many of the young talents in the area.

At that point Marcus gave Winston a nod, after which our driver left the room and returned a few minutes later with my tote bag and guitar saying, "I will wait for your call Sir", and that he left again to wait in the underground.

I was then given a quick tour of the studio we would be using. The control room was very well equipped with a 48 channel mixer and MIDI as the flagship of the Armada.

The dead room as they called it, was appointed with Cedar above and some kind of foam below to soak up unwanted sounds.

The Live room was about the size of a standard classroom, with a large stage area joining the wall that separated it from the dead room. I appreciated the design of the studio right away, and made a mental note for future use.

The two professionals at this point began to talk together about many things and it seemed that I was quickly forgotten. As I listened however to their conversation, I began to realize that they had engaged in many previous conversations concerning how to best package and market this ministry.

It seemed that Chris had already seen many videos of the ministry from Canada, and had a good sense of what it would take to promote and make it a household item.

After a time I took my guitar to the opposite end of the room took it out of the case and saw that I had brought telecast. I sat for the next half hour at least getting acquainted with the guitar and singing softly to the Lord.

Sometime later the conversation lapsed, and Chris got on the phone to the receptionist, and a short time later she appeared with coffee and donuts after which, the conversation resumed. Following another span of conversation Winston was called and I was safely delivered to my hotel.

It had been a long day and I was really too tired to do anything. So I turned on the TV and turned to the quietest movie I could find.

Not for the sake of finding some entertainment, but rather, for the purpose of having some tertiary sound. Some white noise if you prefer, to soften the voices of the night, when even the smallest sound is magnified.

As tired as I was, I felt it necessary to talk to my father in heaven, concerning the plans being made concerning the ministry.

He assured me that he was in control of it all, and that if he could get me into every home in America somehow, then he also would have a place in every home. I saw the sense in that and fell asleep soon after.

The phones were quiet the following day, giving me an opportunity to master the looping features on each of my pedals. I found the demos on YouTube, which helped immensely, and saved me weeks of trial and error.

To make it easy on myself I started with a I, IV, V, progression in the Key of G. Nothing fancy, just a standard A A B A gospel chorus format.

I had some difficulty at first, but once I learned how it all worked, I was able to begin playing a major pentatonic scale over the changes.

I was a little hesitant at first, not really knowing what to do. You know what they say, "when in doubt."

So I did what anybody else would do, I looked it up on YouTube.

After watching a few videos, I had the idea and went back to playing the scale over the changes.

This time though, I started by playing just one note at a time, letting each one a ring out for a full four count.

When I had gone through the scale several times like that I started using two notes, and then three. I soon began to get a feel for two and three notes phrases, and my confidence began to grow from that point.

Not long afterwards fell I began to hear a note of discord that would not go away no matter what I tried. That meant there was only one solution, I powered off computer and the G5, and went downstairs for a well-earned brunch.

The hostess was beginning to get used to me by now, and always seemed to have a table for two tucked away in a quiet corner for me, far enough away from much of the bustle.

All the way down on the elevator I have thought of eggs Benedict, but looking over the menu I opted for a western omelette with a stack of buttermilk pancakes, ham, bacon, sausage, and toast.

An hour later I made my way back to my room after enjoying a wonderful breakfast and leaving a generous tip. Back in the elevator, I began to think about my guitars once again.

I had been using the telecaster, and made up my mind to try the 60s strata for my next session. Back in my suite I powered up the computer and the G5 once more, and took my amp off of standby.

Having set my ringer to vibe only, and keeping it in my shirt pocket assured me that I would not miss a call if I use the headphones.

I had paid $160 for this set of headphones, and was not disappointed. The tone and the crisp clean sound of the music was all that I had hoped for. I played a number of songs for about a half hour getting used to the feel of the guitar and how to strum it without turning the volume up and down every time I swept the pick too far in one direction.

Now that I was comfortable with this instrument I hit play on the G5 and I began to play the loop I had pre-recorded previously. I immediately appreciated the difference in tone between the two guitars, and began to work with the scale as I had previously. As I did so I made a note to self to practice this way at least every other day.

I guess the second thing that I really noticed was the difference of the action, and how the Stratocaster played differently from the Telecaster.

Sometime later I notice that my fingers of my fret hand were beginning to hurt, and looking at my watch, I realized that it was after 5 PM. Taking a break and finding nothing on the TV, I decided to take a nice hot shower and immediately felt much better. A change of clothes and a quick shave my electric razor, and then back to the restaurant to try their Salisbury steak, with a generous portion of mashed potatoes and gravy.

Back upstairs and it was prayer time. I was really beginning to enjoy the looping feature on the G5, but felt I should give the others a chance as well. My first priority though, was prayer.   As outlined previously, this was once again a time of quieting the inner chatter, silencing the self-talk, and feeling after God.

I truly have no idea how long I sat for the Lord before I fell asleep. Still and all, it was after 10 AM when I opened my eyes again.

Splashing cold water on my face in the bathroom and dragging a comb through my hair, donning casual close grabbing the cell phone and room key, I was on my way back downstairs for another Western breakfast.

I was on my 3rd cup of coffee when I noticed that the atmosphere of the restaurant had changed somehow.

Up until this morning people had ignored me, and cheerfully carried on with their incessant babble. Sitting in my quiet corner I had always heard the peoples chatter and casual conversation to be much like a babbling brook.

Today however people were beginning to notice and pay attention. At first I thought maybe I need to check my wardrobe.

Going through my basic wardrobe (shirt, shoes, and jeans) I quickly realized it was something different. My next guess was that they had been to a bookstore lately and saw my picture, and so note to self, "advertising works".

With that in mind, I knew that I would have to get used to this sort of thing as my new norm. But this was New York, where the people are used to seeing celebrities daily.

As I thought about it I began to realize that those who showed interest in me were my public. And I soon began to see that if I related to them openly all would be well, and for the most part some boundaries would be observed.

Finishing my coffee, I left my customary tip and made my way back to my suite.

My room had been cleaned by the time I got back, I was always grateful for that courtesy.

It had been my intention to become familiar with the other looping devices, that as I thought about it I realized I needed to un-box the PA system as well as the Tascam 36.

I wasn't sure I was that ambitious. Still and all, some wise guy had once said, "the longest journey begins with a single step". The recording unit was closer (not to mention smaller) so I started with that.

It also proved to be the least amount of work. Once through the packing tape the box opened easily, and the unit was easy to remove from the box.

Wrapped in clear plastic and supported on either end to minimize shaking. Just a few seconds were necessary to remove the Styrofoam supports and the plastic wrapping.

A large instruction booklet was also protected inside the packaging, and the power cord had been sitting underneath, and that's all there was.

In the end I was glad to have purchased the instructional video which explained the operation of the unit in greater detail than the instruction booklet. I had also ordered the home recording school which was advertised on the instructional video.

With that done all that was left was on boxing the PA system, which went quickly enough. I had not purchased speaker stands with the system to facilitate easy moving and storage.

After unboxing and removing the protective packaging I began to connect the speakers to the recording unit and quickly deduced that I had failed to anticipate the need for some very important equipment, monitors.

I had no monitors. I could do without speaker stands however monitors were indispensable. An oversight which I would have to correct.

Being pleased with my progress I decided to reward myself by making a fresh pot of coffee, and while that was perking, my eyes fell upon the one thing I had not yet opened the case containing my 70s era Les Paul guitar.

After removing it from its case I ran the patch cord from the guitar to the tuner, and as it was perfectly tuned moved the cord from the tuner to the amplifier.

At first I found the body of the guitar to be heavier and more awkward to handle. But with the properly adjusted strap those issues quickly went away. I could smell the coffee now and set the Les Paul on the stand I had designated for it, and went to pour and doctor my coffee.

Returning from the kitchen I powered up the G5 and turned on the looping feature, this time playing the minor pentatonic scale over the changes. I immediately appreciated the bluesy quality of the notes, and the smoother sound of the guitar.

Waking up my laptop and going straight to YouTube.com. I searched for videos of the Les Paul guitar being demonstrated. After watching one or two videos, I went in search of videos that was show me how to get the best sound from my amplifier and guitar.

Chapter Seventeen

Feeling the need for a break I picked up the remote, turned on the TV and found the Summer Olympic Games being broadcast from somewhere in Asia. I settle back in a comfortable chair, and an hour flew by remarkably fast.

Turning off the television I went back to my Les Paul. This time I began to practice by playing first the major pentatonic scale and then alternately the minor pentatonic scale. I so enjoyed playing in this manner that I realized that it was time for me to learn new strumming patterns.

This of course meant going back to YouTube where I found all manner of strumming patterns, riffs and runs, and various other techniques. I spent the next three hours working to develop the skills which had been made available.

A little after six pm I started to feel severe hunger pangs. Looking up the local attractions on the house IPad, I found directions to a jazz club called the Blue Note in the west village. I looked it up on my laptop, and saw that casual would be the dress code. Half an hour later I was in a taxi and on my way to the west village.

I didn't stay the whole night, just an hour or so to grab a snack and listen to some Jazz great that I had never heard of before I sat down and to eat and listen.

The stage was a low rise, one step platform big enough for five to six people. The backdrop consisted of two sets of velvet drapes (or so I imagined) blue under purple, and the Blue note sign where they met. The food, the people, and the music made for a wonderful ambience, and a great crowd.

Sitting comfortably in the back seat of the checker cab, I knew in my heart that I would be happy to be good. Yes, I was confident in who I was, where I was going, and most importantly, where the Holy Spirit was leading me.

In truth, at the end of all things there would be one question for me to answer. Did I walk with my God in integrity?

I suppose the Holy Ghost was impressing this thought on my heart at that moment. If that was so, it seemed to me like my father in heaven was telling me what was really required of every soul who accepted the Gospel of peace.

But ... I digress. We pulled up to the hotel about an hour later. Marcus and Chris pulled up just behind us, and I was happy to see a familiar face.

Up in the suite, we talked about my participation in an afternoon healing service the following day. I felt it be fine, and commented that I would welcome the opportunity. The event would be broadcast live on Christian television, and would be used to promote the upcoming book release.

Chris asked about the equipment that was set up, and I explained that I was getting acquainted with the new guitars, as well as the looping feature on the G-5. I saw him looking at the Tascam 36, and a moment later he asked me to show him what I had been working with.

I told him not to expect anything fancy, but was happy about the possibility of working with another musician. I powered everything up, and then started to play over the changes. A few minutes later, he grabbed one the guitars, and on my nod began to solo over the changes as well.

While he did so, I saw an opportunity to add in a bass line. After jamming for about ten minutes, he stopped and powered up the Tascam unit. Once he had connected everything to his satisfaction, we started playing again while he recorded various tracks.

We added bass and vocal tracks, and then he mixed it all together. After two hours, being very pleased with himself, sent the recording to his studio via Wi-Fi, and began to make some calls, giving instructions to those on the other end.

When he was done, it was time for a good meal, and he took us to his favorite place for Italian. Another venture into the west village. Somewhere in our dinner conversation, Chris began to explain that the music was flowing on a level somewhere between cool tunes and hot jam session that would get a lot of hits online.

It was at this point that Marcus, smiling like the Cheshire cat, handed Chris his IPhone and told him to hit play. We did not noticed that he had walked around and filmed the entire session.

Another flurry of excitement and instructions given over the telephone. The music video would be on the net by the time we finished dinner. The two of them were rather pleased with the jam session, and were soon lost again in exploring the possibilities.

Even though I was forgotten, (again) I was compensated by the arrival of my plater of Spaghetti and meatballs and gave my full attention to enjoying that. I caught bits and pieces of the conversation, but soon lost the thread again.

By the time Winston had arrived to take me to the event on the following afternoon, we had to change to a larger venue, and add an evening service also.

Churches and other groups, as well as individuals from all over the state had seen the video, purchased tickets, and by noon, more 25,000 people were making their way to the location of the Musical Miracle Ministry.

As a result of getting acquainted with the different guitars for the past few days there was no question that for the Ministry, I preferred the warmer tones of the Les Paul. It should be no surprise to anyone then that I had Winston drive by the music store where we had purchased the first one, and obtained another Les Paul the same year and model, only this one was a deep crimson in colour.

Since I was already at the music store I purchased a good set of monitors as well as other accessories, including a 50 foot cable for my guitar. Yes I realize, that I could have just picked up a wireless system, but that would come later.

Putting the equipment in the trunk of the limo except for the guitar that is, and we were off to the concert venue.

I had asked Winston as we were driving how his family was and his smile said it all, they were just fine.

When I asked him where the venue was and he told me, that we would be at a concert venue downtown that had a 50,000 person capacity. It was probably at this point that I realized the Garage Band days were gone for good.

I wrote the rest of the way in quiet prayer asking God what he wanted to do for the people. All he would say was, "open your mouth and I will fill it". From that response I understood he was telling me just to get there and he would do the rest.

A short time later Winston pulled up to the visa the VIP entrance where we were met by the stagehands that Winston had called for to carry my equipment onstage and have it ready for me.

When I was shown into the VIP room (which was really more like a lounge) I found that a number of singers and musicians already gathered and waiting for their call.

Most of them seemed to be acquainted in one way or another, which was not surprising. When I walked into the room, everybody stopped talking.

Seeing that I was momentarily the center of attention, I looked around with a smile and said, "Hey! I'm Tommy, you know the deaf dumb and blind kid, I'm here to testify. "

Everybody laughed at that and the awkward moment passed, and it seemed that I was accepted as they begin to introduce themselves one by one. As they did so they went back to what they were doing before I walked in. Finding a place to sit near a TV monitor, I began to watch the show and was really quite impressed.

The singers and the pastors that had gathered together to take part in this event were really quite good. I realized that working with Chris was a real blessing.

It was really quite a workout for the stage manager making sure everybody was on stage of their proper time. The VIP room gradually emptied leaving me as the last one to go on stage.

I had been appreciating the talent that God had given these men and women, when suddenly I heard my own music being played and I knew that any minute the stage manager would be there for me. He appeared a moment later and I was ushered backstage to wait for my queue.

I was handed my red guitar, and was given instructions on where to stand etc. then I was on stage and the show was mine.

Chapter Eighteen

I was suddenly appreciative of the cordless microphone that they had outfitted me with. This was the biggest stage that I had ever been on, and I could see that it would take a great deal of movement back and forth to speak to this crowd.

As I took the stage a wholly hush filled the venue. I began by strumming the guitar softly pedaling between the D cord and Dsus4. I felt the anointing of the Holy Spirit began to well up within me and I began to sing, "There is a river".

By the time we had sung it through twice, people were beginning to weep in their seats. Others began to raise their hands and worship, while others simply hung their heads.

It was not long before the Holy Spirit began to say to me, "I'm ready to heal the people". I asked him where he was starting, and he replied by saying "on the left-hand side close to the stage, about halfway up there is a little boy who has leukemia which has recently gone out of control.

He is wearing a blue bandana I'm touching him right now. Over on the right-hand side, there is a woman in the third row who lost her faith early in life, and now the doctors have told her she has terminal cancer and does not long to live."

"She is wearing a green dress with a red sash, when she comes up on stage I'm going to heal her. In the wheelchair section there is a dark skinned man wearing a black hoodie. He has a fake bomb strapped to his chest.

I want you to call him up on stage and expose him gently. I will tell you what to say when he comes up on stage." All I could do was to nod and say "yes Lord".

I pointed out the man in the Lord had indicated and asked for him to be brought up on stage. As expected he stayed in the wheelchair still hoping to deceive. The others had not reached the platform by the time his wheelchair was brought up on stage, and so I thought to deal with him quickly.

I spoke to him as the Holy Spirit instructed saying, "Young man, your family was deceived by a false prophet when you were just a child. Your parents suffered much loss and damage at his hands. From that time you have held me responsible says the Lord, but I have stood with you and your family all these years, and delivered you out of worse harm."

At this time I leaned in closer, putting my hand over the microphone and said to him, "You came here tonight thinking that this was a sham, and that I was a false prophet. Your purpose was to bring fear and expose the lies".

"Nonetheless, God wants you to know that he has not left you or forsaken you."

"In fact by the end of the week the man that deceived your family will restore everything that he took from you many times over. Your family will be restored to wealth and dignity."

"You have a fake bomb attached to your chest, this ends here and now. You need to get out of this chair and forgive God in your heart. You can leave quietly and only the three friends that came with you tonight and myself will know of this. If not then you will stay in this wheelchair as long as you live."

As the young man looked up at me in surprise and wonder, as I leaned back, speaking into the microphone once more for all to hear saying, "God wants you out of this chair in ten, nine, eight," and that was all it took.

When I said eight he jumped to his feet, ran across the stage and back, spoke into the handheld microphone saying, "I'm healed! Thank you, thank you God!" He shook my hand profusely and ran off the stage.

This of course brought the crowd to its feet in a thunderous ovation of praise to the Lord, which lasted several minutes. The Holy Spirit told me to extend my hands towards those who were left in the wheelchair section, and say be loosed of your infirmity.

When I did this there was a sound of a mighty roaring wind, and every wheelchair was empty within a matter of seconds.

Those who had occupied the chairs seemed dumbfounded. They could not comprehend how they got to their feet, or why they were still standing.

Those who had MS, or some other debilitating affliction were completely healed. As they looked up at me I signal for them to come up on stage.

I had guesstimated approximately three hundred, or three hundred and fifty wheelchairs. At one minute per person, that meant 5 to 6 hours of testimonies. Clearly I had to think quickly.

As they were coming up I instructed the altar workers to separate them by category. Those who had MS or cerebral palsy, some sort of spinal injury or amputation, and so on.

Once they were all on stage and separated into groups or categories, I instructed them to see the altar workers before they left the service, and leave their contact information. I also asked them to bring letters of confirmation of healing from their doctors.

I then called for the altar workers and have them form rows of 50 on the stage, then went through the rows gently tapping each one on the fore head, and one by one they dropped to the floor, slain in the spirit. Dealing with them in that way took approximately 10 minutes, which made a good diversion for the crowd.

As soon as the stage was cleared again, my two cancer patients had finally made it to the platform. As they stepped towards me the Holy Spirit said, "Loose them from their infirmity." When I obeyed the Holy Spirit they both seem to faint and fell to the floor unconscious.

As they fell to the floor I was instructed to call all of those who had cancer, diabetes, arthritis, or glaucoma to the altar area. About 2000 to 3000 people came to the altar area.

This time I called for all of the pastors and their ministry teams to come and get the people's information.

As the pastors were coming, I loosed the people of their infirmity and spoke healing in the name of Jesus. I instructed the pastors to separate the people into groups.

Those who were Christians and those who were not, those who had cancer, arthritis, diabetes, or glaucoma. To get their contact information as well, and to lead them through the sin's prayer if necessary.

Chapter Nineteen

With that looked after I called for the singers and musicians, and by then Chris was on the stage ready to take the lead, and the stage manager got me and my guitars back to the VIP room where Winston was waiting to drive me back to the hotel.

Winston help me to get everything upstairs, and when I asked him if he knew what was happening for the evening he replied that he wasn't sure, but that somebody would call me within the hour. I thanked him for his help, and gave him a generous tip.

With my equipment safely upstairs, it was time for my next priority, supper! In the restaurant downstairs I was shown to my usual table, where I ordered the chicken cordon blue.

The staff was getting to know me by now, and the waitress brought me a tall glass of cool water with a lemon wedge.

As expected, Chris Chatterton called me within the hour. That made it just about 8:00 PM. He began by saying he was aware of the time. Went on to say that he would ordinarily cancel the service for the night and just do it tomorrow, but they had sold tickets and the people with their.

"No worries" I told him, "just give them some music, make some announcements and send somebody to get to pick me up. What kind of response did we get from the crowd this afternoon?" I asked him. "Well, the crowd has nearly doubled, does that tell you anything?"

I couldn't help laughing and said, "Well brother I guess if it ain't broke, we won't try to fix it".

That seemed to put him at ease, and he began to chuckle. "All right then, same format. I'll see you soon."

Back of stairs I had time to shower and put on fresh clothes. The phone rang as I began to put my shoes on to go downstairs, and it proved to be the driver that Chris had sent to collect me.

The sun was beginning to set outside, and as I exited the building it came out from behind a cloud, bathing the entrance and myself in golden light. My chariot for the night was as shiny black stretch limo.

The uniformed driver was a tall portly middle-aged man who was courteous and professional, accustomed to getting VIPs to and from their destinations and comfort. On the telephone he had introduced himself simply as Jackson.

And I thought to myself, "Someday, I will find somebody who can explain to me why chauffeurs have only one name."

As I reached the sidewalk he opened the door saying, "good evening Mr. Thomas, would you like your guitar in the boot?"

I responded by saying "Thank you Jackson, I'll keep it with me this time."

"As you wish Sir." He replied as I was getting comfortable on the seat cover and then he closed the car door firmly but gently.

At that point the Holy Spirit began to talk to me concerning his health saying, "Jackson has been sick for a long time Son."

"Father God" I asked, "what is the problem?"

"His kidneys are failing, and he can no longer afford dialysis" was the reply. I thought for a few minutes, choosing my next words carefully and asked, "What do you want to do father?"

Hesitating just briefly he instructed me to first ask about the kidneys, and then we could continue the conversation.

This was a relatively new turn in the conversation. My curiosity won out in so I pushed the intercom button.

"Yes Mr. Thomas?"

"Jackson, do you mind if I ask you a personal question?"

"That depends Mr. Thomas."

"How is your health Jackson?"

"My health is fine sir."

"Your kidneys Jackson, how are your kidneys?"

"My kidneys are fine sir."

"Thank you Jackson".

"Yes Sir."

After a moment or two the Holy Spirit was speaking to me again.

"Well son?"

I took a moment before answering and then responded by saying, "he's not ready".

"That's right" came the response.

"Is there any way to help?" I asked.

The Holy Spirit responded by saying, "we just did".

Before I could respond in any way the car stopped, the curbside door was opened and Jackson was saying, "We have arrived Sir."

"VIP entrance Jackson? I asked.

"Yes sir".

"Thank you Jackson".

"Yes Sir. Mr. Thomas?"

"Yes Jackson?"

"Thank you Mr. Thomas."

"Yes Sir."

The smile on his face and the light in his eyes spoke volumes. In my heart I said "father?"

"Yes son?"

"Thank you Sir".

Chapter Twenty

I was then ushered in to the VIP lounge were several other musicians from the afternoon session were again present. I greeted them and they responded by saying together, "Tommy!"

I have to admit that I felt like one of the crowd. That I somehow belong in this setting. I commented on parts of their performances that I had truly enjoyed, and that I asked those who had already been on stage with this crowd was like.

Just as before the room emptied and filled up again and before I knew, it was my time to shine.

The only thing I changed was not being introduced. Instead, I began to play from backstage as the previous group was leaving.

Not strumming hard or fast, but just gentle fingerpicking in the Key of G. Before I had taken three steps I began to feel the Holy Spirit flowing like a mighty river.

I began to sing we exalt thee and hosanna in the highest, and I knew that the Holy Spirit was healing people all throughout the stadium. After a short time I change keys again and began to sing like the fire. I spoke of God's redeeming grace, and man's great need of such. The Holy Spirit gave me scripture after scripture speaking of the love of God and the purpose of God for mankind.

I would have open the altar but there was no need. People were streaming to the altar weeping and crying out to the Lord, it was wonderful to be a part of this. All I could do was call for the pastors and the ministry teams to come and minister to the people.

I called for the music teams to come and lead the people in worship as thousands were repenting of unrighteousness, and being restored and healed right where they were.

I found Jackson waiting for me in the VIP lounge, and in a few minutes were making our way back to my hotel. I began to feel more than a little peckish as we drove and so I asked Jackson if he knew of a place where I could get some take-out pizza and pasta. He said he knew just the place that was 10 minutes out of our way.

It didn't look like much of a place, it was just a take-out join really. But there was a steady stream of patrons who looked very satisfied as they left with their orders. Having a feeling that I would have company when I got home, I ordered two extra-large supreme pizzas.

Two large orders of spaghetti and meatballs, with extra meatballs, two large orders of lasagna, one large order of pepperoni lasagna, and having sampled the wings, I also took Four dozen of those. As an afterthought, I also added a couple 2 L bottles of Pepsi.

Jackson help me get everything to the door of my sweet wife sent him for his help and gave him $100 tip, and then he disappeared quickly down the hallway and into the elevator. I had just closed the door and put everything on the table, when the phone began to ring. Marcus and Chris were on their way over and were wanting to talk.

10 minutes later they were falling from the lobby saying they would be up shortly. And as promised they were there and just a couple moments. They were happy to see the pasta, the pizza, and especially the wings.

They said they had a few friends coming over who were wanting to meet me, and was I up to it. I assured them it would be fine and they apparently phone downstairs for people to start coming up. I could not help wondering how many a few meant. I thought it best to have them all arrive together, and said so to Chris.

He seemed to relieve and got on his phone immediately. Minutes later stream of visitors began to pour in through the now open door. I stopped counting at 20, allowed myself a sigh of resignation, then smiled and told him to phone for more pizza.

In all there must've been nearly 100 people in my hotel suite. People just kept coming in. Not long after that there was a steady stream of people delivering food.

Chapter Twenty One

There were pastors and musicians, media moguls and politicians, reporters and camera men. I dared to imagine that things were going just a little better than originally hoped.

I had seen this sort of thing in the movies. I remembered that in these situations people were expected to schmooze. So I grabbed the paper cup that was filled with Pepsi and began to schmooze.

I need to say up front that there were far too many faces and names to remember. I walked around pretending to sip my Pepsi and whenever somebody looked at me I would give them my name and we would chat for a moment. Sometimes they would give me a business card, then go back to their previous conversation.

I think that I was on my third round through my apartment when Chris came and directed me through the crowds to a relatively quiet corner where they had set up a small table and chairs for more personal ministry.

I was pleased with this because my pockets were quickly becoming filled with business cards. Crist asked if I he could refill my cup, and then he asked if I had had a chance to eat anything. What I smiled my answer he nodded rushed off and was back in minutes with refreshments.

While I was replenishing the funeral in my tank, Chris began to explain what was about to happen. When I indicated that I understood he moved away quickly, but was soon back with half a dozen reporters and as many cameramen. He then signaled to a group of three photographers to join us as well.

I began by telling them that this was all new to me, and asked if they had any advice to give me before we began. In response, the cameras were turned off momentarily and basic instructions were given. At my nod, the cameras were turned back on and pictures were taken, and the interview began.

The interview was brief but focused and the reporters did their job well. As I was answering the last question, the Mayor of the city was brought forward. There was a formal introduction and handshake followed by a flurry of flashes by the photographers.

He then made a brief speech, and spoke to me about meeting him at City Hall the following afternoon where he would officially welcome me to New York, present me with the key to the city. There was another handshake an exchange of smiles and another flurry of camera flashes.

It went this way for the next half hour. As I was formally introduced and greeted and photographed with some of New York's elite. After this the cameras and reporters vanished, and there was the three free spite where I was able to take a bathroom break and replenish my energies. That it was back to my little corner of the world.

As if on cue, the lights and cameras returned, more instructions were given while makeup was applied, and then I was introduced and photographed with the movers, shakers and delete of the city's entertainment industry.

After another short break there were more introductions and photo ops with some of the most influential members of New York's Christian community. With that the media moment was over and the cameras were packed away.

At this point some of the reporters and cameramen came and shook my hand and told me that for a newbie I had done quite well.

Not long after the place was quiet and empty except for Chris, Marcus, and a small army of housekeeping staff from the hotel to quickly clean and restored my suite to its pristine serenity. For which they were generously rewarded with tips and autographs from the three of us.

With everyone finally gone and order restored, the three of us sat comfortably for a moment or two basking in a moment of silence.

I broke the silence by asking if there was any food left. This was followed by an exchange of glances and the silent agreement that each of us was hungry. Suggestions were made but in the end it was unanimously agreed that burgers were in order.

Soon after we were at a Red Robin restaurant in the city that never sleeps. It was half pound burgers all the way around, and huge stack crispy onion rings, washed down by a gallon of iced tea. I believe that it was unanimously agreed that this was not the time to discuss the events of the last few days.

There would be a time to discuss and analyze the events that this was not that time. Staying purposely away from any topic that even sounded spiritual in nature, we talked about everything else. About planes and trains and automobiles mostly. An hour and a half later we had exhausted every topic we could think of including ourselves.

Marcus offered to have Winston drive me home. I declined his offer, and as he and Chris departed for their own homes I did what anyone else in New York would do, I hailed a cab and went home.

Because my hotel suite had already been cleaned up on the do not disturb sign on the door handle outside, found the movie channel and adjusted the volume, and promptly fell asleep on the bed.

I woke up several hours later to the sound of running water and bright sunlight illuminating the room. Something troubled me about that statement and then I realized, it was the sound of running water. Getting up off the bed and following the sound until I found the source, I asked Marcus what was going on.

He laughed saying, "Gawd! For a kid from the prairies you sleep like the dead!"

"Well" he said as he continued, "you can relax a bit, the meeting was moved back until 2 PM, so you have some breathing room."

"Why was it moved back?" I asked.

"On account," he said.

"On account of what?" I asked as I played along.

He was laughing now, "on account the Mayor slept in after being at some social event last night."

"So, I'm Troubled about one thing. If you knew the meeting was moved back, why are you here, and how did you get in?"

"I told the manager that you were late for an appointment with the Mayor." He replied as he nodded towards a few envelopes on the table, "and you have a few pieces of correspondence."

I went over to the table to see what they were, and then noticed a pile of about twenty medium sized boxes piled up by the door. "And these boxes?" I asked.

"That would be a few more." He said with a grin. "C'mon, let's get some brunch! Chris will be ordering for us if we don't make a move! "

Down in the Restaurant we found that Chris had pulled a number of tables together, and it looked that we had the beginnings of a small entourage.

I recognized a number of the musicians and singers from the V I P lounge of the previous day. When I greeted them, they responded with a unified "Tommy!" The others were corporate heads, publishers, magazine editors, and Christian community leaders. These were some of the major players in the film and entertainment industries. As I moved towards an open seat at the table I asked the Lord if this was the fulfilment of his plans and purpose for me. After a moment of silence he answered me saying, "No Son, today we are stepping out of the shadows. Now the real work begins."

Notes

Thank you for reading this story. To find other Titles from this author, or to give a review, go to www.amazon.com/author/drjspeters

47487418R00099

Made in the USA
San Bernardino, CA
31 March 2017